Sam

Amelia

David

Timothy

24.

Robert

Amanda

Belinda

Moss

Marcus

*For Claire and Lucy*
NM

*For Gillian*
AA

ORCHARD BOOKS
96 Leonard Street, London EC2A 4RH
*Orchard Books Australia*
14 Mars Road, Lane Cove, NSW 2066
1 85213 601 4
First published in Great Britain in 1994
Text copyright © Nicola Moon 1994
Illustrations copyright © Alex Ayliffe 1994
The right of Nicola Moon to be identified as author and Alex Ayliffe as illustrator
of this work has been asserted by them in accordance with
the Copyright, Designs and Patents Act, 1988.
A CIP catalogue record for this book is available
from the British Library.
Printed in Belgium

# Lucy's Picture

Nicola Moon
*Illustrated by* Alex Ayliffe

ORCHARD BOOKS

"My Grandpa's coming to tea today," said Lucy.
"That's nice," said Mrs Kelly. "Now, sit down.
We're all going to do some painting."

"Can I do a picture for Grandpa?" asked Lucy.
"Of course you can," said Mrs Kelly.
Lucy looked at the big sheet of white paper in front of her.
"Can't you think what to paint, Lucy?" asked Mrs Kelly.
"What would Grandpa like?  Something nice and bright?
Look at those lovely colours!"

Lucy looked at the red and the yellow and the
sky blue paints. "They're not right," she said. "Can I
use the glue? Can I stick things on to make a picture?"
"You mean a collage? Of course! But you'll have to
sit at another table. There's not enough room here."

Lucy took her paper to an empty table in the corner. She went and found a pot of glue, some scissors, and the box of scraps.

Lucy loved Mrs Kelly's box of scraps. She liked plunging her hands deep in the box and feeling with her eyes shut.

Lucy started her picture. She cut some soft green velvet into curvy mounds, like hills, and stuck them on the paper. She made a lake out of blue shiny stuff, and put it in between the hills. Then she found some flowery dress material.

"Grandpa has flowers like this in his garden," Lucy told Mrs Kelly. "He likes the blue ones best because they have the nicest smell." She cut round the flowers and stuck them in little clumps along the edge of the lake.

At playtime Lucy was too busy to play. Instead she
collected twigs and leaves and then she found two small
feathers! She filled her empty juice
cup with sand from the sandpit.
At last it was time to go inside.

Scrapbox

Now Lucy was very excited about Grandpa's picture. She made him a tree out of the twigs and the leaves, and stuck the feathers on the end of a branch. Then she spread some glue in a long winding band over the hills, and scattered sand over the glue to make a path.

"My Grandpa's got a dog," Lucy told Mrs Kelly.
"She's called Honey because that's what colour she is."
When Mrs Kelly wasn't looking Lucy cut off a tiny
piece of her own hair and stuck it in a shape like a
dog lying under the tree.

Scrapbox

"That's lovely, Lucy," said Mrs Kelly, when it was time to stop. She put Lucy's picture safely on the side to dry along with all the paintings.

Lucy couldn't wait until home time. She hadn't seen Grandpa for ages.

Her mum was waiting as usual, but today there was
someone with her.
"Grandpa!" Lucy nearly knocked him off his feet.

"I've made you a picture, Grandpa.  Look . . ." Lucy grabbed
her blind grandfather's hand and guided it over her picture.
"These are hills, and here's the road . . ."
Grandpa touched the picture carefully.  "A tree.  A bird.
And what's this?  It feels like your hair, Lucy."
"That's Honey!" said Lucy, smiling.
"You are clever.  And what a lovely surprise.  It's the best
picture I've ever seen!"
said Grandpa.

Lucy

And hand in hand, Grandpa, and Lucy
and her mother walked home for tea.

Sara

Gillion

William

Katie

Sally

Daisy

Henry

Jonathan